W9-ATR-217

Hoang Breaks the Lucky Teapot

Rosemary K. Breckler　　Illustrated by Adrian Frankel

Houghton Mifflin Company　Boston　1992

For my grandson, Christopher Wayne Lasater
And wishing Jeremy Nguyen a long, happy, prosperous life

—R. K. B.

To my family and for Joe

—A. F.

The author gratefully acknowledges the assistance of Mrs. Nhan-Lan
Nguyen; Master Dam Luu and the nuns of Duc Vien Buddhist
Community Pagoda, San Jose, California; Ms. Jessica Huong Dang;
Mr. Anthony Vnu, director of the San Jose Vietnamese Chamber
of Commerce; Ms. Sharon Do; Mr. Inh Ranc Tran of the San Jose
Vietnamese Community Center; and the Vietnamese seniors at
St. James Senior Center for Asians in San Jose.

The illustrator wishes to extend special thanks to Phi-Bang Nguyen.

Library of Congress Cataloging-in-Publication Data

Breckler, Rosemary, 1920–
    Hoang breaks the lucky teapot / Rosemary K. Breckler;
illustrations by Adrian B. Frankel.
        p.   cm.
    Summary: When a Vietnamese boy breaks his gia truyen, a
teapot which houses *May Man*, good spirits, he tries to repair the
damage in order to keep away evil spirits and bad fortune.
    ISBN 0-395-57031-X
    [1. Vietnamese Americans—Fiction. 2. Family life—Fiction.]
I. Frankel, Adrian B., ill. II. Title.
PZ7.B744Ho   1992   90-24265
[E]—dc20   CIP
                     AC

Text copyright © 1992 by Rosemary K. Breckler
Illustrations copyright © 1992 by Adrian B. Frankel

All rights reserved. For information about permission
to reproduce selections from this book, write to
Permissions, Houghton Mifflin Company, 215 Park Avenue South,
New York, New York, 10003.

Printed in the United States of America

HOR   10   9   8   7   6   5   4   3   2   1

During the late 1970s, thousands of Vietnamese fled in small boats after the communist Viet Cong conquered their country. Of those people who survived a long, dangerous trip, many settled in the United States. Often arriving with nothing but the clothes they wore, they tried to begin new lives in this unfamiliar country.

This is probably how Hoang (HWONG), the main character in *Hoang Breaks the Lucky Teapot*, and his family would have arrived. Most likely they would not have been permitted to take anything onto the dangerously overcrowded boat, but I wanted Hoang to keep his *gia truyen* (za TREN). Perhaps he hid it inside his quilt. In keeping with the animistic* beliefs of many Vietnamese, this special teapot is believed to contain *May Man* (my MUN), good fortune and good spirits, which keeps away bad fortune and evil spirits.

Hoang's *gia truyen* had been passed from father to son through many generations on his mother's side of the family. Because he was the last surviving male on that side, however, Hoang inherited it from his mother's mother.

As the family's great treasure, the *gia truyen* was placed on the *ban tho* (bahn TAH), their memorial altar, as soon as they had a new home. Almost every Vietnamese family has a *ban tho* in a private part of the house. It is used for prayers and for the remembrance of ancestors and family members who have died. On the anniversary of the death of a family member, water or tea is poured from the *gia truyen* into its matching cup and left on the *ban tho*, along with fresh fruits and flowers, to show respect for the ancestor.

A recently arrived family such as Hoang's would have only a few items on their *ban tho*. By their altar you will see a portrait of Hoang's great-grandfather, painted by Hoang's mother, and Hoang's *gia truyen* and matching cup. Centered under the painting is a *bat nhang* (baht NYANG), a brass mug decorated with dragons. A layer of rice in its bottom holds sticks of incense. Beside the *bat nhang* are red candles in brass candlestick holders, also decorated with dragons.

The dragon is used as a symbol on the *ban tho*, in temples, and during Tet, the Vietnamese New Year's celebration. It is regarded as both a powerful protector and authority figure and a destroyer and punisher, and thus is both honored and feared.

When Hoang meets a dragon and breaks his *gia truyen*, *May Man* is no longer there to protect the family, and *Xui Xeo* (sooey SELL), bad fortune and evil spirits, runs free in their house.

—Rosemary K. Breckler
San Jose, California

*In an animistic religion, people believe that all inanimate objects contain good or evil spirits to be avoided, confused, or appeased.

Hoang wasn't much taller than the kitchen table, but his imagination was taller than the house.

One day as he stood in the kitchen, holding a blue ball in his hands, he saw a dragon hissing steam on the table. The dragon hovered just behind his mother.

BAM! He threw his blue ball at the steaming dragon. Ma cried out in alarm.

There on the floor lay Hoang's *gia truyen*, the lucky teapot his grandmother had given him on the scary night when they left their home in Vietnam.

He remembered his grandmother saying, "This teapot holds *May Man*, the good fortune you will need to keep you safe from evil spirits on the dangerous journey to your new country." Now it couldn't even hold water!

He watched Ma sadly gather all
the pieces into a white bowl and
place the bowl on the *ban tho*, the
family's altar. To Hoang, it felt like
she was saying goodbye to *May Man*,
maybe forever!

Was *Xui Xeo*—bad fortune and
evil spirits—now running free in
their house? Would it find them?
Would it destroy this home in
America they loved so much and
chase them back across the scary sea?

The day became dark, darker, cold, colder. Ma turned on the lights. She put a sweater on and then put one on Hoang. Was *Xui Xeo* hiding the sun? Would all the days now be clothed in cold and gloom? Hoang shuddered. Somehow *May Man* had to be brought back into the house. But how?

Then he knew. He'd make a new *gia truyen* and maybe *May Man* would move into it and chase *Xui Xeo* from their house!

Hoang went outside to the puddle where he often molded things from mud. But the mud was so hard he couldn't even chip it. His head hung down as he went back inside the house. To warm them, Ma made tea in an old, chipped teapot.

When Ba came home, a strong wind howled through the door. It was colder than any wind Hoang had ever felt. "Winter is coming," Ba said, rubbing his hands together.

Hoang wanted to hide when Ma showed Ba the pieces of the *gia truyen*. Ba threw his hands into the air. "The *gia truyen* shattered!" Ba thundered. "Now our first winter in America will surely be a monster."

Hoang wanted to ask about this monster called Winter, but his parents looked too worried. He backed away from them and peered out the window. Their sidewalk and the street were disappearing under drifts of white. Winter was erasing their world!

Did Hoang have to fear not only *Xui Xeo*, but this monster as well? He had to fix his *gia truyen*. But it was dark. And it was late. After soup Ma put Hoang into his bed, patting his quilt around him.

In bed, Hoang's mind swirled. He saw butterflies searching for the right flower. But no good ideas bloomed. He saw *Xui Xeo* and Winter running through the house, turning everything that was sweet sour, making everything that was warm cold.

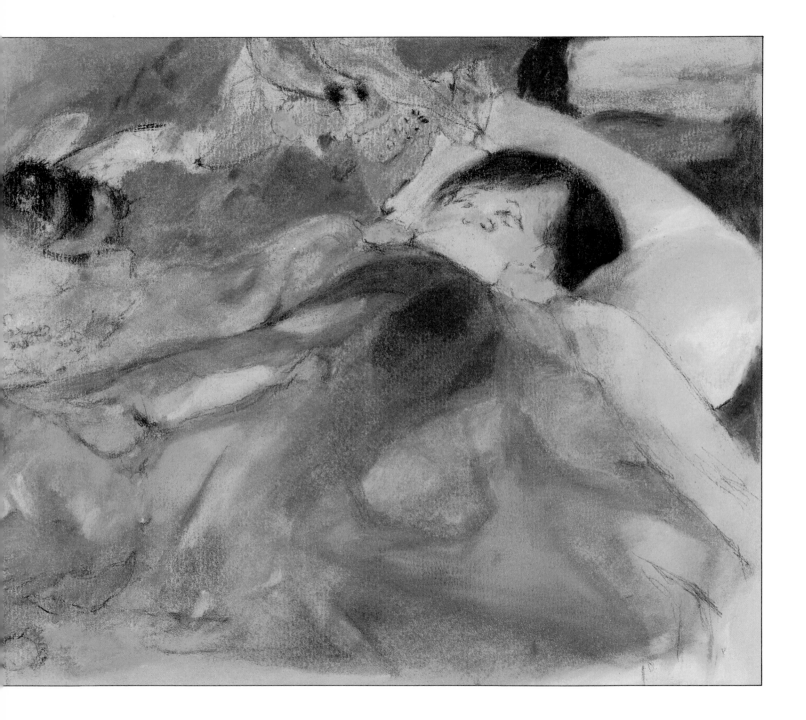

When at last he fell asleep, he dreamed that a giant dragon was shoving him into a huge teapot and pouring ice-cold water on him. He woke up and wrapped his face in his quilt—but the quilt was angry at him for breaking the *gia truyen*. It refused to make him warm. Hoang decided it was time to bring *May Man* back to their home for good.

When he was sure that Ma and Ba were fast asleep, Hoang got up and tiptoed to the *ban tho*. He lifted the bowl down and carried it to the kitchen table. He spread the *gia truyen* pieces on the table.

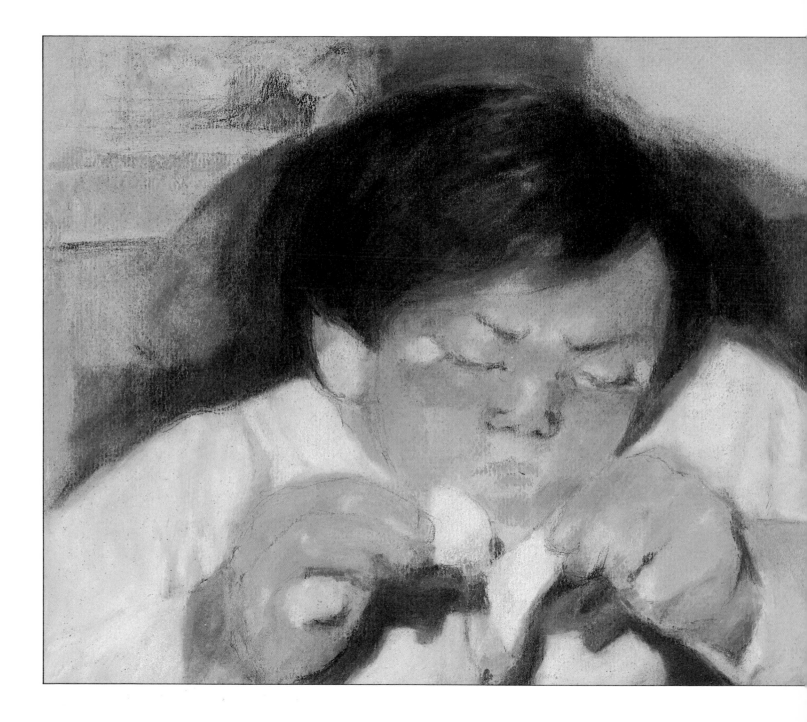

He tried gluing the teapot together with honey and bits of rising bread dough, but the pieces fell into a glumpy lump.

He found his father's glue, but it wouldn't hold the pieces together in a teapot shape either.

Then he saw Ma's paints up on a kitchen shelf. They gave Hoang an idea. He climbed up and got down all the little pots of many colors and the brushes of different sizes.

Hoang wasn't sure how to match the designs that still shone on the pieces of his cherished *gia truyen*, but he mixed some colors and he tried them on the old, chipped teapot.

As the night grew colder and lonelier, he looked often over his shoulder to be sure *Xui Xeo* wasn't creeping up behind him.

At last he thought the old, chipped teapot maybe looked like his *gia truyen*. With care and respect he set it on the *ban tho* with the hope that *May Man* would forgive him and be tempted to hurry back into it.

Tired as he was, he gently gathered every piece of his *gia truyen* into the bowl and hid it behind the painted teapot.

He got into bed with a sigh.

Morning arrived dark and cold. When Hoang awoke, he sat up in surprise. Ma was standing in the doorway, smiling!

Then he saw that she was holding the painted teapot in her hand. Hoang smiled back. It seemed *May Man* had recognized the new *gia truyen* and had come back into their home.

Franklin Pierce College Library

00069199

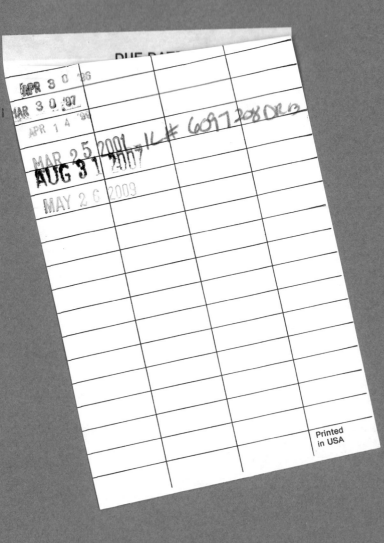

DUE DATE

APR 3 0 96

MAR 3 0 97

APR 1 4

MAR 2 5 2001   IL# 6097208DR6

AUG 3 1 2007

MAY 2 6 2009

Printed
in USA